THE MAGIC FOUNTAIN

The Magic Fountain

By H.R.H. Princess Gloriana

The Story Behind the Book
By Roger McGough

Illustrated by Philip Hopman

RED FOX

A Red Fox Book

Published by Random House Children's Books
20 Vauxhall Bridge Road, London SW1V 2SA

A division of Random House UK Ltd
London Melbourne Sydney Auckland
Johannesburg and agencies throughout the world

1 3 5 7 9 10 8 6 4 2

First published by The Bodley Head Children's Books 1995

Red Fox edition 1996

Printed and bound in Hong Kong

RANDOM HOUSE UK Limited Reg. No. 954009

ISBN 0 09 943391 5

CHAPTER ONE

'I have just wrote a story,' said the Princess.

Her Royal Highness Princess Gloriana had swept into the Great Hall of the Palace and announced the news to the assembled court.

(As you well know, of course, she should have said, 'I have just written a story,' but grammar was not her strong point. Nor was spelling or punctuation, or good manners, or anything for that matter.)

'I have just wrote a story, and I want it published.'

Everybody cheered and clapped wildly.

'Congratulations!' cried the King.

'Clever girl,' cooed the Queen.

'Might we not hear it?' asked the Lord Chancellor.

'Very well,' said the Princess, and cleared her throat. 'It is entitled: *The Magic Fountain* by HRH Princess Gloriana.'

'Oooh! *The Magic Fountain*,' echoed the courtiers. 'Sounds good… mmm… exciting.'

The Princess began:

'*Once upon a time there was a beautiful princess. One day she met a handsome prince and before you could skin a rabbit they got married and lived happy ever after. You may go.*'

CHAPTER TWO

The Princess closed her notebook, lowered her eyes modestly and raised a hand as if to stop the applause.

Dutifully, the applause began, blushed, and faded away.

The King turned to the Queen, who turned to the Lord Chancellor, who turned to the Princess.

'Very.. er... good, Your Highness. Very... er... Perhaps, a little short!'

'Nonsense,' said the Princess. 'Most stories what I read are far too long and boring.'

Many a courtier nodded in agreement.

The King leaned towards his daughter and said gently, 'Your story is called *The Magic Fountain* my dear, but... er... there doesn't seem to be a fountain in it.'

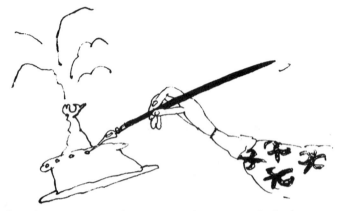

'Then the drawer can draw one,' snapped the Princess impatiently.

'Darling...' this time it was the Queen, 'Darling, the bit about skinning a rabbit...'

'What about it!'

'Well, darling, don't you think, perhaps it's just a teensy weensy bit cruel?'

The Princess tutted, 'It's a dead rabbit, it won't feel a thing, not a sausage. And any road, you are all being horrid and stupid because this is the best story what has ever been wrote.'

'I agree, I agree,' said the Lord Chancellor soothingly. 'It's got everything; romance… adventure… a dead rabbit. It's got a beginning… a middle, and er… oh, and one final question, at the end it says, "You may go". Who may go? The reader do you mean?'

'Of course,' said the Princess. 'Once he's read the story, he can remove his cap, bow very low and then get back to work where he belongs.'

'I just love the ending,' trilled her mother. Then added, 'But, what if the reader is a woman?'

'Then she curtsies,' said the Princess and flounced out of the Hall.

CHAPTER THREE

The very next day, the best illustrator,

the best bookbinder

and the best publisher in the land

were summoned to the Palace.

The Lord Chancellor made a long and passionate speech about literature and the challenge that lay before them. About how lucky they were to give their services free and help produce the most exciting book the world had ever known.

By the time he had finished they were wild with enthusiasm and impatient to get on with the job.

Then he showed them the story.

CHAPTER FOUR

The Great Day came at last and the Princess's book was published. Flags were hung from every window. Bands played in every town square. There were street parties and carnivals, and everybody dressed up and laughed and feasted and had the most wonderful time.

Nobody, however, bought the book.

(Well, to be honest, that isn't strictly true. A few avid readers and royalists bought a copy, but within minutes of leaving the bookshop, they were back at the counter demanding their money back.)

After the Great Day came the Miserable Months, as the books piled up in the shops gathering dust. To boost sales, bookshop managers tried everything,

'Free Fountains'

'Free Wellingtons'

'Buy a dozen copies, get one FREE'

'Buy one copy, get a dozen FREE'

But all to no avail . . .

The Princess locked herself in her room and refused to come out, and the illustrator fled the country to join the French Foreign Legion.

CHAPTER FIVE

The King and Queen it must be admitted were not great readers. They preferred outside pursuits (like pursuing things outside, for instance, usually on horseback).

However, as loving parents they wanted their only child to succeed in her chosen profession, and so they asked the Lord Chancellor to think up ways of encouraging people to buy her book.

'The people must have freedom of choice,' declared the Lord Chancellor.

'Indeed they must,' agreed the King.

And so the following day a law was passed giving every householder the choice of either:

a: buying a copy of *The Magic Fountain*.

or b: going to prison for six months.

CHAPTER SIX

Within weeks *The Magic Fountain* headed the best-seller lists and stayed there. Suddenly the Princess was in great demand on arts programmes and on TV chat shows.

Her book was turned into a musical by the court musician and simply everybody bought the T-smock. (Although, how many actually read the book remains something of a mystery.)

The publishers were delighted and were soon at the Palace requesting another blockbuster. A sequel to *The Magic Fountain*, a follow-up, anything in fact, that the royal pen may deign to scribble.

The Princess was flattered and set to work at once. But, try as she might, she couldn't put pen to paper.

Seated at her desk in front of the mirror and looking every inch the writer, she tried.

Every day for a whole week, sometimes for as long as half an hour, she would sit gazing at herself, but the well of inspiration, that fountain of magic, had simply dried up.

CHAPTER SEVEN

'Writer's Block,' the royal physician called it and prescribed pineapple chunks and plenty of rest.

Word wizards were called to the Palace;

wise witches with the gift of the gab;

tellers of tall tales;

dream-jugglers,

even plumbers, but all failed to unblock her.

18

To mourn the loss of her fragile gift the Princess wore only black and her courtiers were instructed to do the same.

A fun palace it was not.

CHAPTER EIGHT

By now, copies of *The Magic Fountain* were on sale all over the world, although people preferred to read about the author than read the book itself.

Photographed on horseback or beside her swimming pool, the Princess was a much loved and admired figure.

One of her biggest fans was Prince Waldo of Glockenstein, a poor country whose only industry, the manufacture of chicken-clocks, was short-lived, owing to the invention of the Swiss cuckoo-clock some weeks later.

The Prince's hobby was collecting. He had the largest collection of fishbones and exit signs in Europe, but his newest hobby was collecting autographs.

Already he had three – his mother's, his father's and the man behind the counter of the autograph-book shop.

'If only I could get Princess Gloriana's autograph,' he mused, 'my collection would be complete!'

The very next day he left for Grandonia.

CHAPTER NINE

To improve his mind as he travelled across wild and dangerous countryside, Prince Waldo tried to read *The Magic Fountain* but lost track halfway through and ended up deep in the forest.

He decided to set up camp for the night and while crumpling up some old newspapers to make a fire, he came across an article about the Princess.

It told of how she was unable to write another story, and this made him very sad.

'There must be lots of exciting stories in the world,' he thought,
as suddenly, a hoard of fierce Visigoths burst screaming out of the
darkness and carried him off to their mountain stronghold.

'Interesting anecdotes. Don't you agree?'
'Well, if you say so,' said the talking bear, who had rescued him
in the nick of time, from being skinned alive.
'But what's an anecdote?'

'It's simply a matter of observing the world around you,' he explained to the mermaid, as she hauled him from the shipwreck and carried him safely to the desert island.

'Although I suppose the difficult part...' he confided in the friendly dragon who flew him over the snowy mountains of Iceland, 'is writing it all down.'

By the time he reached the Palace, he knew exactly what he was going to do.

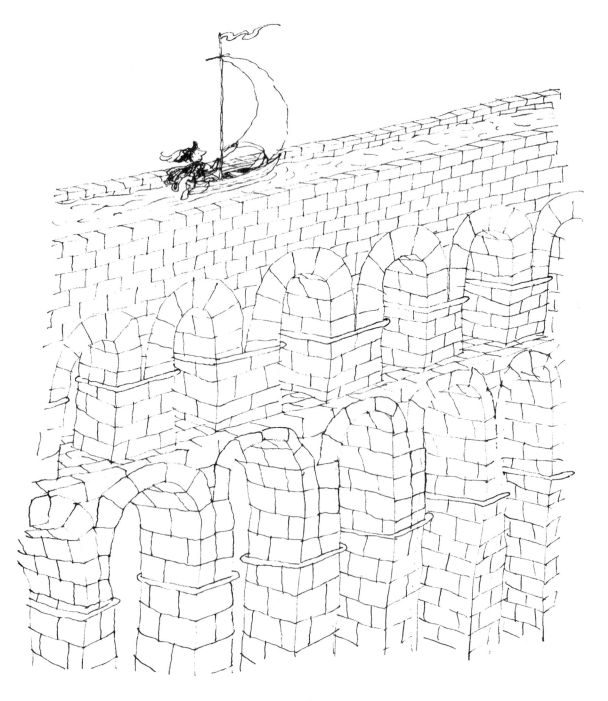

CHAPTER TEN

'Prince Waldo of Glockenstein,' announced the Lord Chancellor and stepped aside to allow the Prince into Her Royal Highness's writing chamber.

Clutching his autograph book to his bosom, the Prince strode manfully towards the Princess who paused from doodling on the table cloth.

He bowed.

'Your most loaded... I mean, *gracious* Highness, I am a great admirer of your work. Where I come from you are regarded as the greatest writer since... since...' (he struggled to think of the name of a writer) '... since Mozart.'

'Mozart? Wasn't he a piano-player as well?' asked the Princess, 'Or what?'

'Indeed,' replied the Prince, 'and a very good painter too.'

'Oh, I wouldn't half wish I could draw a painting or play a musical instrimint,' sighed the Princess.

'No no no,' said Waldo, warming to his subject. 'Mozart, Shakespeare, Rembrandt, they all spread their talents far too thinly. A bit of this, a bit of that. Whereas a true genius... like yourself.'

(Had the Princess not been blue-blooded she would have blushed, as it was, she turned a light shade of puce.)

'A true genius ploughs a solitary furrow.'

The Princess, wondering why the conversation had turned suddenly to the subject of ploughing, began to hum, out of tune, a little tune.

'A pretty melody,' ventured the Prince, 'Mozart perhaps?'

'Rembrandt,' corrected the Princess sternly. 'Now, what do you want?'

CHAPTER ELEVEN

What he wanted was to marry the Princess.

What he wanted was to get his hands on the Royal Fortune.

What he wanted was to send money back home where there was much poverty.

What he wanted was to have a son who would succeed to the throne.

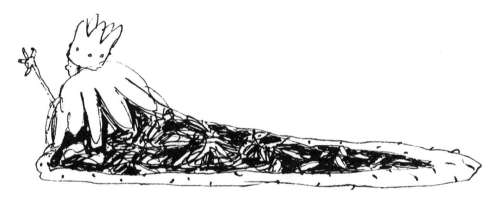

What he wanted was to unite the Kingdoms of Glockenstein and Grandonia.

'What I want,' said the Prince, 'is your autograph.'

CHAPTER TWELVE

Having been granted the Royal Scrawl, Waldo thanked Her Highness and pointed to the bookshelves that lined the walls.

'A magnificent library,' he remarked.

'Yes, I own the most hugest collection of *Magic Fountains* in the universe, all personally signed.'

Prince Waldo knew that this was his opportunity and he seized it.

'It would be truly wonderful wouldn't it, if you were to write another story, entitled, for instance, *The Amazing Adventures of Prince Waldo*, which was even better than *The Magic Fountain*.

He watched the colour drain from the Princess's face and her bottom lip tremble.

'Of course, I can't write for toffee, but I have a wonderful idea for a story and I wondered, I just wondered...'

He watched the colour return and the lip untremble.

'Wondered if... you'd like to have it for your long-awaited second book?'

The Princess opened wide her eyes and held out her arms 'Oh please, please tell us it. Tell us it now.'

'There's just one thing,' said Waldo. 'One small favour I must ask in return.'
'Anything,' said the Princess. 'Anything.'

The Wedding was planned for the very next chapter.

CHAPTER THIRTEEN

> ♔
>
> *Their Royal Majesties*
> *The King & Queen of Grandonia*
> INVITE YOU
> *to the wedding of their daughter*
> *H.R.H. Princess Gloriana*
> *to*
> *H.R.H. Prince Waldo*
>
> AT THE PALACE NEXT SATURDAY 2PM.
>
> *be there, or be square! (or, be headed)*

Everybody was invited...

Including Prince Waldo's best friends...

And as for the wedding, it had everything...

Church bells.

Guard of honour.

Golden coach.

Prancing white horses.

Handsome couple.

Page boys.

Procession.

Wedding cake.

Champagne.

Speeches.

Usual sort of thing.

Bridesmaids.

(Oh, and confetti.)

CHAPTER FOURTEEN

The Great Day came at last (again) and the Princess's second book was published. Flags were hung from every window. Bands played in every town square. There were street parties, and carnivals, and everybody dressed up and laughed and feasted and had the most wonderful time.

This time however, everybody bought the book. (The penalty for not doing so being death.)

CHAPTER FIFTEEN

The Prince and the Princess fell in love and had many children, and Waldo's dream of uniting the two countries came true. Happiness and prosperity reigned.

And the story?

The Amazing Adventures of Prince Waldo by HRH Princess Gloriana.

'Once upon a time there was a beautiful princess. One day she met a handsome prince and before you could wash a pair of socks and hang them out to dry, they got married and lived happy ever after. You may go.'